Air Dair

Fust

Booker Pomes

Written and Illustrated

by

A.B.Wyze

ISBN 9798698130673

2020

PREFACE

Any similarity between characters mentioned in this book, either alive or dead is purely coincidental. Apart from the one about my mum, that is.

The first poem I attempted to write in the Northamptonshire dialect is the first one featured here. A work colleague of mine who was 'not of these parts' got married to a local girl. He told me that one of the things that attracted him to her was her 'way of saying things.' He was particularly fascinated by the way she pronounced the word electricity as lectric. The poet in me immediately set to work and Thu Bit Thut Din't Git Lit was written that very afternoon. This is one of the poems that is based upon fact. The illustration accompanying the poem is based upon the Co-op store which was situated at the bottom of Hove Road in Rushden. The jitty that ran alongside that shop was not lit and neither was the bottom end of Hayden Road where it led to. There were times when you could not see your hand in front of your face.

The second poem on offer is purely a made-up affair. As soon as I decided to compile enough material for a book I simply sat down and began making stories up.

The third poem is also straight out of my imagination. Alleyways in Northamptonshire are frequently referred to as jitties and I simply wanted to include that euphonism in a poem.

I rarely have a complete plan when I begin writing poems. Air Arleen was a case of writing the first verse and then facing the challenge of achieving a satisfactory ending. My late sister was called Eileen (Arleen) but this is most certainly not about her.

Wi Wenupter Lundun does have an element of fact about it. Most local people of my generation would have no trouble at all in remembering Birches Coaches and their regular run into the capital.

Poem number six is mainly based upon fact. The roads in Oval Crescent where I was born were known as Hitler's Revenge. It was said that they were partly built by Italian and German prisoners-of-war. Exactly how much truth there is in that story is anyone's guess, the roads were concrete in construction and during the cold winter months, any snow would hang around for up to a week after it had disappeared throughout the rest of the town. Not that us kids minded in the least.

I attended Newton Road Infants and Junior school. Not Nubdee Nowair is loosely based upon the one time I ran away from school.

I was born at number five Oval Crescent. For most of my life, I have lived in Rushden. My wife and I moved away in 2009 to live for seven years in Hunstanton. Upon moving back to Northants we lived for about eighteen months in Raunds before coming back to Rushden. While in Raunds we did use the doctor and we did use the shortcut and believe me it *was* as 'steep uzzeck!'

Styutome Mum is unashamedly about my mother. Both her and our dad believed that a mother's place was at home. The poem speaks for itself.

The final poem has a certain amount of truth to it. After moving back to Rushden and setting up home in Gloucester Crescent we sort of inherited a cat. It belonged to the family next door. This cat made a habit of visiting the lady who lived next door on the other side. When she sadly passed away the cat adopted Wendy, my wife, as her surrogate mum. That is where the fact ends. I composed the first verse whilst walking back from the shops and then went off on a flight of fancy.

Thanks for taking the time to read this short piece. If I am honest, whenever I come across a preface in a book I almost always skip it. I hope you go on to enjoy the poems and drawings but if you struggle with any of the text in my interpretation of the Northants dialect I have included full translation towards the back of the book.

Thanks again.

THU BIT THUT DIN'T GIT LIT

Wen lectric cumter Ruzzdun
thuwurra bit thut din't git lit.
Ureownd thu bakkerthu co-op
juss deown thu rowd uh bit.
It wuh blakkerun Calcutter
in itz veree blackist bit
un yew cud chork
on the worls deown thair
un not see wot yewed rit.

Un on cumin bak
frum thu pickchers
we ad tuh walk thru it.

We'd juss bin tuh see
Flash Gordun
un thu klaymen in thair pit.

Ikun tellyuh we wuz wurried
not jus wurried
we wuz frit.

Areownd thu bakkathu Co-op
in thu bit thut
dint git lit.

IKWOLLERTEE

Oi dorn't wonner scairyuh
nair, that woon't bi fair,
but Mooreen air airdressuh's
dooin blowks air.

Shizz got thu wurd yewnersecks
ritt onner shop.
Oi sed I din't loike it
she adder roite strop.

Shi sed thut thu barbuzz
wuh neow inthu parst
un singulsex salunz
thay coon't nevvuh larst.

Shi sed uppin Lundun…
shi sworrit me duck,
thut yewnersecks salunzer
commun uzz muck.

Shi sedditz ikwollutee,
this ent no jowk.
Wotguzz fer the wummun
sairm guzz fer the blowk.

Oh gel I wuh fumin
oi stood frum me chair.
Oi giverutannuh
fer dooin me air.

She yeld. "Itz tooshillin…"
er akculs wuh rizz.
Oi sed, "Mi ole man
paizzuh tannuh fer izz."

Oi tuk olt me kidz
un oi sed thair'n then.
"Wotz gud fer the wimmin
iz gud fer the men."

Oi sed od be bakthair
fer woddit wuh wurth.
Bak wen ikwollutee
meks men gi burth.

THRU THU JITTEE

"Om gooin' thru thu jittee Duck
it dorn arf sairve me legz.
Om gooin' tuh thu Co-op
furra duzzun free rairnge eggz.

Oh nair they ent fuh me meduck
om geddin' um fuh Fred.
E luvs a cuppla chukkie eggz
fuh shairin with izbred.

O yair, gel if yuh wonner foo
oi dorn't moind geddin sum.
Thair freshist eggz areound yuh no,
still warm frum chikkinz bum.

Om gooin' thru thu jittee tho
woll we still gotsum loight.
Oi'd nevuh goo deown their meduck
in miduller thu noight.

Oh nair, I dorn't goo forrem gel
them eggz mek me feel ruff.
Thay blockupp orl yuh artrizz gel
with that thair clestrul stuff.

But Fred sez thair pure evven
oh eez roight ruliguss, Fred.
E sez thudeel be eetin um
long aftuh e iz dedd.

E rekunz them thair doctuzz gel
thay med that clestrul up.
E eetz un drinkz juss wot e loikes
o yair e loves tuh sup.

Oi wurree furrim gel oi do
oh wotz e gunnathink
if e getz up turrevven
un thair ent no beertuh drink?

Well, kent stopporl day chopsin' gel
oi reerly gotta goo.
Me list iz longerun me arm
itzarf day clozin' too.

Oi'll drop yurreggzin corse oi will
oi'll troy tuh get bak kwik.
Nair, pay me wenyer goddit gel
oi'll puddit on thu TICK!"

AIR ARLEEN

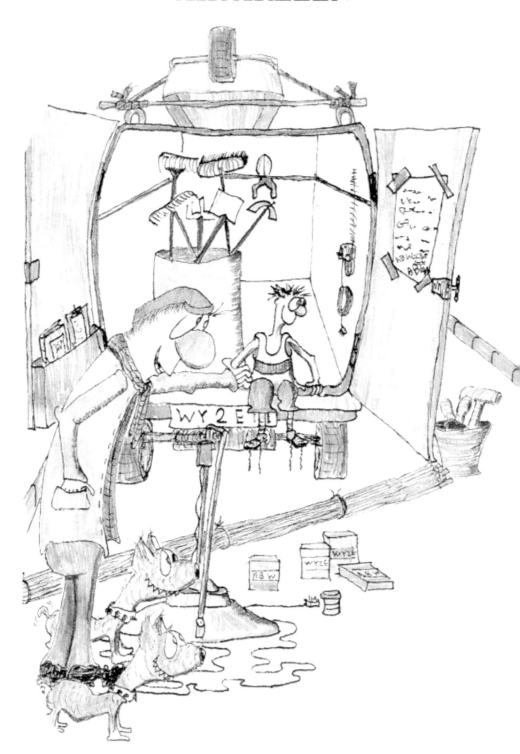

Air Arleen
shizzuh lass sheeizz
shi dornt much goo fer rools.
Shi spenter penshun…
orl uvvit
un bort sum
gardnin' tools.

Er bloke, that Freddy wossizname
e wennun poptiz clogs.
E nevuh lefter much e dint.
E backed three leggid dogs.

Buttee ad this ullotmunt see,
it ent too fur frum teown.
Un Arleens gonnun took itton…
One mumf corsts arfer creown.

Neow blokes dornt goofer
  gardnin gels
    it rubzem up wrung way.
Thayeld uh meartin
  deown thu club
    so thaycud evv their say.

Thay supped a bit
    thay scoffed sum grub
thay fild thu plairce wi smowke.
              Then staggudome
                  tuh tell thair wives
                      thut wimmin
                          wurra
                              jowke.

Bud Arleen's Freddy wossizname...
yair im wots neow elswair
well eeyad
sum cunecshuns see
iz nefyew
wuh thu Mair.

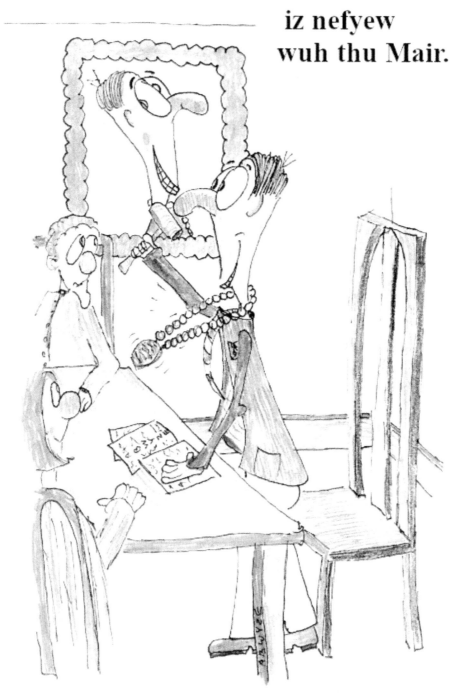

Und up thu counsul weeyulls turned,
thu mair e addiz say.
Air Arleen gotter plot shi did
wiv not uh thingtuh pay.

Ullotmunt blokes wuh madduzzel
they thort thut it wern't fair.
But nunnovem dair speark owt lowd
in cairse thay crawsed thu mair.

So Arleen started plarntin stuff
uzziff shi wour possessed.
Shi earvun filled uh bukkitt up
un groo sum wartuh cress.

Neow Arleen's Freddie wossizname
oowin thu grevyard lay
e adder littul book e did
wot e kepp idduway.

Itwurra booker gardnin tips
Arleen din't avverclew.
Shi fownd thu book uppinizz shed,
oh man, thu thingzzee noo.

Un soon er beenz wuh too foot tall
wile blokes cud not bi seen.
Thubosser thurrullotmunt
e popped reound tuh see Arleen.

"I juss popped in tuh seeyuh gel
juss cumter tek uh look."
Budarleen noo woteed cum fer…
eed cumter git thu book.

Eyung urrownd e adsum tea
eyung urrownd sum mor.
Eyofferd Arleen discairnts
attiz in teown ardwair store.

Un orlthu toime is rowminise
wuh checkin owter shed.
Eeadter find that gardnin book
thu wun wotz rit be Fred.

Budarleen wurra canny lass
shi med airt cupsertee
til bosser thurullotmunt left
juss buztin fer uh pee.

Thu bosser thurulotmunt
wurruh locksmith nown uzz Glyn.
That noight e wenter Arleen's shed
un eeserlee browk in.

Eeadder torch ucorse e did
e shonnit fer uh look.
Un unduneeth uh piler rags
e fownd thugardnin book.

Izz fairce littup morun thu torch
izz mairf wuh parched un droide.
E opunned up thu book e did
un shonthu tor chinsoide.

Izz frote it medder skweekin sairnd
azzee lukked thru thu book.
Izzands wuh cowld un swetty
un izz armzun legz juss shook.

Thuwernt no ritin ennywair
septon the owpnin pairge.
Uh singul frairse wottee juss noo
wud orntim furrun airge.

E redthu frairse owt lowd e did
yewadter feyull fer Glyn.
It sed…
'Juss digunole fer veg,
un then juss purrumin!'

WI WENNUPTER LUNDUN

Wi wennupter Lundun
wi din't mek no fuss
Wi paktup sum sarnizz
uncort Burchizz bus.

Wi went deown thu emmwun
that bus dinnarf shift
Wi sorsum itchicuzz
thay din't giddalift.

Wi stopton thu emmwun
fer tekkin' a leek
mi missuzz got grubowt
shi'd packed furraweek.

But sumfoke ad nuthin
so weeadter shair,
juss fish pairst or ayzlitt
thay din't simter cair.

Wi got deown ter Lundun
un godder roight scair.
Thu plairse itwuh teermin'
wi foke evreewair.

Thay lukked atuzz toorists
loike weewurrin zoo
un thay wurrorl torkin'
weeyant godder cloo.

Thay torked orl that cotnee
issorful turreer
loike sum forrun lairngwidge
it sowndid reel kweer.

Io sedter me missizz,
"Necks toime wi goo owt
Oi ent cummin' Lundun
uh that thezz no dowt.

Oi ken unnerstandem
their torkin' too kwik.
Un their lukkin' atuzz
uzziff weerorl thick.

Nair, thaykun kip paliss
un that Lambuth Wark.
Oi ent cummin' bakeer
til thay lernter tork!

REMMUNISSIN'

Wi dintev carzzin air strit
notwen oi wuh juster kid.
So wi plaird futborl in thu rowd
iss juss wot weeorl did.

Them rowds wuh bilter conkerete
it meddem reelee good.
Cus thair wuh loines ucrawsum
wair thu gowlie wudda stood.

Weeorl umagunned wid bin pict
fer bess teem in thu land.
Wal septer corse on Sundizz
wen me dad sed itwerband.

Air dad e wurn't ruliguss,
dint goo church no blummin' eck.
Buddee seddon thu Sabbith
weeorl adter sheow ruspeck.

Wi dintave soopumarkitz
sep the Co-op oi serpowze.
Un eow me mum fed sevin kidz
juss God inevvun nowse.

Mi dad wurktin uh factree
mekkin' bootz n' mekkin' shooze.
Un thu wuh lowdzer factrizz
it wuh blummin' ardter chooze.

Air owse wurroned be cownsul
tho wi trettit uz airown.
Wi dintav tellervishun
un wi nevvurad uh fown.

Buddorl thu toime uz we groo wup
air pairuntz roolz wuh set.
Wid orluss trett air nairbuhz
az wid orl loike tuh bi trett.

Oi no tudday thut medersinz
uh bedder crawse thu bord
un evree wun az carzun fowns
un ollerdizz ubrawd.

Oi loike tuh remmuniss izorl
iss wot us owld foke do.
Unwen yuh git tuh mi airge
yull bi remmunissin' too!

NOT NUBDEE NOWAIR

Thurrent not nubdee nowair
ov looktun looktun lookt.

Me teechuz gunner kill me
me goose iz gudduz cookt.

Shisent mi tuh thurroffiss
om lorst unorl ulown.
Ov cumturruh dussishun
oi rekkun oll goowome.

Thurrent not nubdee nowair
offeel juss loike uh fool.
Me mum ennin thu kichin
om gooin' bakter skool.

Thurrent not nubdee nowair
oi dorn't no wot terdoo
Oi wennun fownd thurroffiss
buddit wurremptee too.

Oi sor thu skool cairtairker
juss gooin' crawse thu yard.
Oi ranowt un oi showtid
oi showtid rearleeyard.

"Thurrent not nubdee nowair,
waird evreebodee goo?"
E sed, "Thurrelpin coppuz
tuh surchureownd fer you!"

UP THU DOCTUZZ

Wen wi goo up thu doctuzz
uh shorcutz wot wi tekk.
Wi goo up thru thu spinnee,
oh gel itz steep uzzeck.

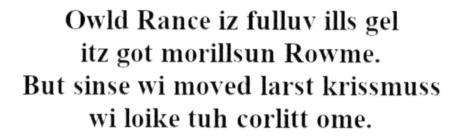

Owld Rance iz fulluv ills gel
itz got morillsun Rowme.
But sinse wi moved larst krissmuss
wi loike tuh corlitt ome.

It texus arfunower
tuh get tuh doctuzz gel.
Un boy thu toime we git thair
we dornt fil verree well.

Thay say it duzzyer gud gel
tuh wark that blummin' far.
But necks toime oi goo up thair
Om tekkin blummin' car!

STAYUTOME MUM

Mi mum nevuh wurked,
uh stayutome mum.
Un moddun mumsay
"Issorite fuh sum."

No mum nevuh wurked,
shi warktuh thu shopz.
Shi wairted wi bags
ut rairny buztopz.

Shi meddup thu far
un shi meddup thu beds.
Wid no reddy meeyulls…
shi meddum instedd!

Wi dintave no fones,
well wun deown thu streart,
un no telervizzun
or puddin up feart.

No woshin mersheens
gaz coppuh wurall.
Uh mangull tuh skweeze
thu wet frumitorl.

Mi mum nevuh wurked
shid swipowt thu roomz.
Wi neveradooverz
juss dusspans un broums.

Wid no sentrulleatin,
wun far in thu grairte
unnot butted crumpits
orl parldon uh plairte.

Mi mum nevuh wurked
budeyeave no dowt
thru luvvun uffekshun
shi tarder salfowt.

NECKSDOR'S CAT

Necksdor's cat dorn't liv necksdor
nair necksdoor's cat livzeer.
Sitz upon air winduhsill
un grinz frumeer tuweer.

Oi ent nodder fanner catz
buddin thad oim ulown.
Oi dorn't loike itz crearpy smoile
it chilzmi tuh thu bown.

Thu missis luvz that cat shi duz,
udorz that skairee smoile
un evree dayull foinder
shoppin' in thu pet food oile

Necksdor's cat dorn eetudome
nair, necksdor's cat eetzeer.
Livzon samun voller vontz
un evun drinkz me beer.

Oi ent nodder fanner catz
uzz io've oreddy sed.
Wurdz wuh sed, quoite angree wurdz
un neow om in me shed.

Eetmee meeyulz earidoo
me woife wuh cleeronthat.
Oi arst er tuh chooze yusee
un shi chowze necksdor's cat

Necksdor's cat sitzon that sill
un grinz deown at me shed.
Necksdor's cat luks fittun wal
un unlioke me… wal fed!

"O summut mussbidun," Oi sed,
"ken't stan thisennnymor,"
Oi foldid up me sleerpin bag
unneddid fuh necksdor.

Me nairbuzz woif izz twoice my soize;
intimmerdairtin sort.
Budeye jussimplee stud me grairnd
un towlder woddeye thort.

"Me missis kikt meeyowt!" Oi yald,
"Oi'm sleerpin in me shed.
Yor bloodee catzin rezidunce,
itz sherrin' moi wiofe's bed!"

Thu wumun lukked me yuppun deown
then grinned frumeer tuh weer
"Oi liokt that cat, Oi reerlee did,"
shi whispud withu sneer.

"But then thu cat frum wundor deown
riplairceter juss loike that.
Un Oi cun say kwytonusslee
Oi luvmy necksdor cat.

Un iffyer dorn't buleeve me
ask me huzzbun," shi then sed.
"Oi'll owpun up thu gairte feryoo
izz sleerpin' innair shed!"

TRANSLATION

All the dialects across the UK vary in their own
way. I have done my best to portray my own in
written form but I am aware that there are
those who might spell things differently. The
local dialect is part of our history; our heritage.
I remember, as a child, attending Newton Road
school in Rushden. Our regular teacher was ill
and we had to endure the teachings of the
dragon-like Miss Scott. She was a stickler for
correct pronunciation and one word in
particular seemed to drive her crazy, that word
was sailor. We were doing a reading exercise
and I was up first. Of course, being a true
'Ruzzdun' boy I pronounced it as 'sailer.' Miss
Scott hit the roof. She had everyone in class say
the word one at a time and if anyone 'slipped
up' she homed in on them and screamed the
word saiLOR at the top of her extremely high-
pitched and rather terrifying voice. For all her
efforts we all went through life embracing the
wonderful Northamptonshire
dialect.

Thanks for reading my
effort.

David Wood
AKA
A B Wyze

Our Dave's First Book of Poems

Written and Drawn by

A B Wyze

Made in Rushden

Barton Seagrave

Stanwick
Raunds
Ringstead

Burton Latimer

Irchester

Wellingborough

Higham Ferrers
Irthlingborough
Finedon
Kettering

Ditchford

Newton Bromswold

Welcome to Rushden

THE BIT THAT DIDN'T GET LIT

When electric came to Rushden
there was a bit that didn't get lit.
Around the back of the Co-op
just down the road a bit.
It was blacker than Calcutta
in its very blackest bit,
and you could chalk
on the walls down there
and not see what you'd written.
And on coming back from the cinema
we had to walk through it.
We'd just been to see Flash Gordon
and the clay men in their pit.
I can tell you we were worried,
not just worried, we were frightened.
Around the back of the Co-op
in the bit that didn't get lit..

EQUALITY

I don't want to scare you
no, wouldn't be fair
but Maureen our hairdresser is
doing blokes hair.

She's got the word unisex
wrote on her shop,
I said I didn't like it
she had a right strop.

She said that the barber
was now in the past
and single-sex salons
they never could last.

She said up in London,
she swore it my duck,
that unisex salons
are common as muck.

She said it's equality
this is no joke.
What goes for the woman
same goes for the bloke.

Oh girl I was fuming
I stood from my chair.
I gave her a sixpence
for doing my hair.

She yelled, "It's two shillings,"
her hackles were up.
I said, "My old man
pays just sixpence for his."

I took hold of my kids
and I said there and then,
"What's good for the women
is good for the men."

I said I'd be back there
for what it was worth.
Back when equality
makes men give birth.

THROUGH THE JITTY

"I'm going through the jitty duck
it doesn't half save my legs.
I'm going to the Co-op
for a dozen free-range eggs.

Oh no they're not for me my duck
I'm getting them for Fred.
He loves a couple of chicken's eggs
for sharing with his bread.

Oh yes girl if you want a few
I don't mind getting some.
They're the freshest eggs
around you know
still warm from chicken's bum.

I'm going through the jitty though
while we've still got some light.
I'd never go down there my duck
in the middle of the night.

Oh no, I don't go for them girl
those eggs make me feel rough.
They block up all your arteries
with that cholesterol stuff.

But Fred says they're pure Heaven
oh he's right religious, Fred.
He says that he'll be eating them
long after he is dead.

He reckons that those doctors
they made cholesterol up.
He eats and drinks just what he likes
oh yes, he loves to sup.

I worry for him girl, I do
oh what's he going to think
if he gets up to heaven
and there is no beer to drink?

Well can't stop all day talking girl
I've really got to go.
My list is longer than my arm
it's half-day closing too.

I'll drop your eggs in course I will
I'll try to get back quick.
No, pay me when you've got it girl
I'll put it on the tick."

OUR EILEEN

Our Eileen she's a lass she is
she doesn't go for rules.
She spent her pension, all of it
and bought some gardening tools.

Her bloke,
that Freddie what's his name
he went and popped his clogs.
He never left her much he didn't,
he backed three-legged dogs.

But he has this allotment, see,
it's not too far from town.
And Eileen's gone to take it on,
one month costs half-a-crown.

Now blokes don't go for gardening girls
it rubs them up wrong way.
They held a meeting at the club
so they could have their say.

They supped a bit they ate some grub
they filled that place with smoke.
Then staggered home to tell their wives
that women were a joke.

But Eileen's Freddie what's his name
yes, him who's now elsewhere.
Well, he had some connections, see,
his nephew was the mayor.

And at the council wheels turned,
the Mayor he had his say.
And Eileen got her plot she did
with not a thing to pay.

Allotment blokes were mad as Hell
they thought it was not fair.
But none of them dares speak out loud
in case they crossed the Mayor.

So Eileen started planting stuff
as if she was possessed.
She even filled a bucket up
and grew some watercress.

Now Eileen's Freddie what's his name
who in the graveyard lay
he kept a little book he did
that he kept hid away.

And it was full of gardening tips
Eileen didn't have a clue.
She found the book up in his shed.
Oh boy, the things he knew.

And soon her beans were two feet tall
while the blokes' could not be seen.
The boss of the allotment
he went round to see Eileen.

"I've just popped round to see you girl.
Just come to take a look."
But Eileen knew what he'd come for,
he'd come to get that book.

He hung around he had some tea
he hung around some more.
He offered Eileen discounts
at his in-town hardware store.

And all the time his roaming eyes
were checking out the shed.
He had to find that gardening book
the one written by Fred.

But Eileen was a canny lass
she made eight cups of tea.
The boss of the allotment left
just bursting for a pee.

The boss of the allotment
was a locksmith known as Glyn.
That night he went to Eileen's shed
and easily broke in.

He had a torch of course he did
he shone it for a look.
And underneath a pile of rags
he found the gardening book.

His face lit up more than the torch
his mouth was parched and dried.
He opened up the book he did
and shone the torch inside.

His throat, it made a squeaking sound
as he looked through the book.
His hands were cold and sweaty
while his arms and legs just shook.

There was no writing anywhere
except for the opening page.
A single phrase which he just knew
would haunt him for an age.

He read the phrase out loud he did,
you had to feel for Glynn.
"Just dig a hole for veg," it said,
"and then just put them in!"

WE WENT UP TO LONDON

We went up to London
didn't make any fuss
we packed up some sandwiches
and caught Birches bus.

We went down the M1
that bus didn't half shift.
We saw some hitchhikers
they didn't get a lift.

We stopped on the M1
for taking a leak
my wife got the grub out
she'd packed for a week!

But some folks had nothing
so we had to share.
Just fish paste or Haslet
they didn't seem to care.

We got down to London
and got a right scare.
The place it was teeming
with folk everywhere.

They looked at us tourists
like we were in a zoo
and they were all talking
we hadn't got a clue.

They talked all that cockney
it's awful to hear
like some foreign language
it sounded right queer.

I said to my missus,
"Next time we go out
I'm not coming to London
of that there's no doubt

I can't understand them
they're talking too quick.
And they're looking at us
as if we're all thick.

No, they can keep palace
and that Lambeth Walk.
I'm not coming back here
till they learn to talk!"

REMINISCING

We didn't have cars in our street
not when I was just a kid.
So we played football in the road,
it's just what we all did.

Those roads were built of concrete
it made them really good
because there were lines across them
where the goalie would have stood.

We all imagined we'd been picked
for the best team in the land.
Well except of course on Sundays
when my dad said it was banned.

Our dad was not religious
didn't go church, no, blooming heck.
But he said on the Sabbath
we all ought to show respect.

We didn't have supermarkets
'cept the Co-op I suppose
and how my mum fed seven kids
just God in Heaven knows.

My dad worked in the factory
making boots and making shoes
and there were loads of factories
it was blooming hard to choose.

Our house was owned by the council
though we'd treat it as our own.
We didn't have television
and we never had a phone.

But all the time as we grew up
our parents' rules were set.
We'd always treat our neighbours
as we'd all like to be treated.

I know, today that medicines
are better across the board
and everyone has cars and phones
and holidays abroad.

I like to reminisce is all
it's what us old folks do.
And when you get to my age
you'll be reminiscing too,

NOT ANYONE ANYWHERE

There isn't anyone anywhere
I've looked and looked and looked.
My teacher's gonna kill me.
My goose is as good as cooked.

She sent me to the office
I'm lost and all alone.
I've come to a decision
I reckon I'll go home.

There isn't anyone anywhere
I feel just like a fool.
My mum's not in the kitchen
I'm going back to school.

There isn't anyone anywhere
I don't know what to do.
I went and found the office
but it was empty too.

I saw the school caretaker
just going across the yard.
I ran out and I shouted,
I shouted really hard.

"There isn't anyone anywhere
where'd everybody go?"
He said, "They're helping coppers
to search around for you!"

WHEN WE GO UP THE DOCTORS

When we go up to the doctors
a shortcut's what we take.
We go up through the spinney
oh girl it's a steep as heck.

Old Raunds is full of hills girl
its got more hills than Rome.
But since we moved last Christmas
we like to call it home.

It takes us half an hour
to get to the doctors girl.
And by the time we get there
we don't feel very well.

They say it does you good girl
to walk that blooming far.
But the next time I go up there
I'm taking the blooming car!

STAY AT HOME MUM

Me mum never worked,
a stay at home mum
and modern mums say,
"It's alright for some."

No, mum never worked
she walked to the shops
she waited with bags
at rainy bus stops.

She made up the fire
and she made up the beds.
We'd no ready meals
she made them instead.

We didn't have phones,
well, one down the street
and no television
or putting up feet.

No washing machines,
gas copper was all,
a mangle to squeeze
the wet from it all.

Me mum never worked
she'd sweep out the rooms.
We didn't have Hoovers
just dustpans and brooms.

She'd bake and she'd iron
she'd polish and dust
and any old problem
me mum had it sussed.

She taught us good manners
she let us have fun.
A housemaid, a teacher
all rolled into one.

And when all us children
got home after school
we knew she'd be waiting
sat there on her stool.

We'd no central heating,
one fire in the grate
and hot buttered crumpets
all piled on a plate.

Me mum never worked
but I have no doubt
through love and affection
she tired herself out.

NEXT DOOR'S CAT

Next door's cat don't live next door
no next door's cat lives HERE!
Sits upon our window sill
and grins from ear to ear.

I am not a fan of cats
but in that I'm alone.
I don't like its creepy smile
it chills me to the bone.

My wife loves that cat she does
adores that scary smile.
Every day you'll find her
shopping in the pet food aisle.

Next door's cat don't eat at home
no next door's cat eats here.
Lives on salmon vol au vents
and even drinks me beer.

I am not a fan of cats
as I've already said.
Words were said quite angry words
and now I'm in me shed.

Eat me meals down here I do
me wife were clear on that.
I asked her to choose you see
and she chose next door's cat.

Next door's cat sits on that sill
and grins down at me shed.
Next door's cat looks fit and well
and unlike ME… well FED!

"Oh something must be done," I said,
"can't stand this anymore,"
I folded up my sleeping bag
and headed for next door.

My neighbour's wife is twice my size;
intimidating sort.
But I just simply stood my ground
and told her what I thought.

"My wife has kicked me out!" I yelled,
"I'm sleeping in my shed.
Your bloody cat's in residence,
she's sharing my wife's bed!"

The woman looked me up and down
then grinned from ear to ear
"I liked that cat, I really did,"
she whispered with a sneer.

"But then the cat from one door down
replaced her just like that.
And I can say quite honestly
I love my next-door cat.

And if you don't believe me
ask my husband," she then said.
"I'll open up the gate for you
he's sleeping in our shed!"

Printed in Great Britain
by Amazon

11352613R00052